Th Little Tiger book belongs to:

_____

_____

For Tess, you light my world... – SM

For all those who love and care for
our beautiful world – CS

Little Tiger Press Ltd,
an imprint of the Little Tiger Group
1 Coda Studios
189 Munster Road
London SW6 6AW
www.littletiger.co.uk

First published in Great Britain 2018
This edition published 2018
Text copyright © Stacey McCleary 2018
Illustrations copyright © Carmen Saldaña / Good Illustration Ltd 2018
Stacey McCleary and Carmen Saldaña have asserted their rights
to be identified as the author and illustrator of this work
under the Copyright, Designs and Patents Act, 1988
A CIP catalogue record for this book
is available from the British Library
All rights reserved

ISBN 978-1-84869-826-0
LTP/1800/2186/0418 · Printed in China
10 9 8 7 6 5 4 3 2 1

I Give You the World

Stacey McCleary

Carmen Saldaña

LITTLE TIGER
LONDON

When you were born, so precious and new,
I searched high and low for a gift just for you.

I searched through the day
and I searched through the night . . .

...till I came across this one –
I think it's just right ...

I give you the world and everything in it.
Come, let me show you –
it won't take a minute . . .

I give to you the dawn's sweet dew,
the morning light just peeking through.
I give to you the spring's soft breeze
that whispers to the tiny seeds.

I give to you the croaking frogs,
the muddy pigs, the sleeping dogs.

I give to you the buzzing bees,
the baby birds – in nests, in trees.

The dolphins dancing just for you,
the whales that sing through oceans blue.

I give to you the sun's warm glow,
the summer rain . . .

...the rainbow!

The clouds through which
great mountains rise,

the eagles soaring
through the skies.

I give to you the falling leaves,
floating down upon the breeze.

The animals, both young and old,
preparing for the winter cold.

I give to you the timid doe,
stepping through fresh fallen snow.
I give to you the day that's done,
the fading light, the sinking sun.

The hooting owl, the pale moonlight,
the stars that sparkle
through the night.

My gift is each and every thing:
each autumn day, and each new spring,

The winter's chill, the summer's laughter,
every season ever after . . .

The wonder, the beauty, the magic unfurled . . .
All this is for you . . .

Give the gift of reading with these wonderful books from Little Tiger...

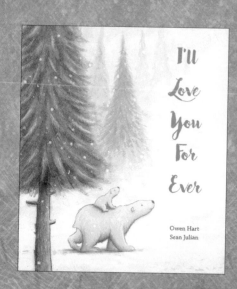

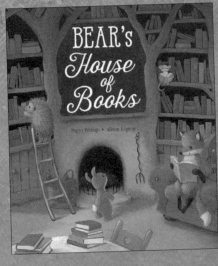

For information regarding any of the above titles
or for our catalogue, please contact us:
Little Tiger Press, 1 Coda Studios,
189 Munster Road, London SW6 6AW
Tel: 020 7385 6333
E-mail: contact@littletiger.co.uk
www.littletiger.co.uk